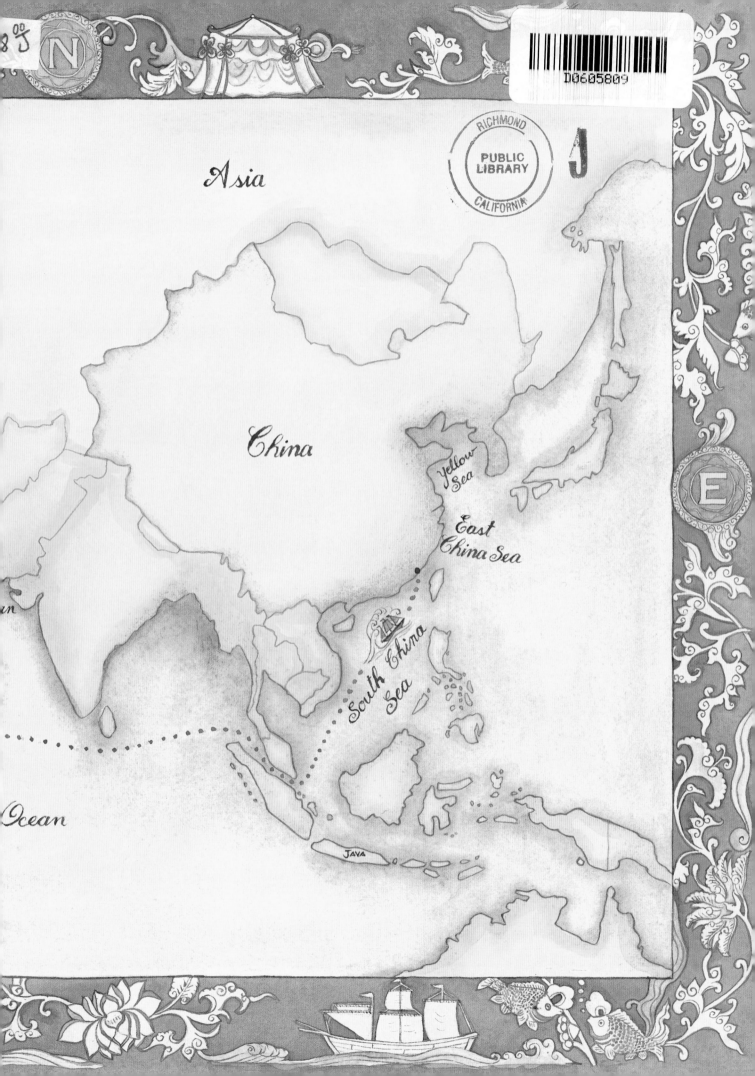

Asia

China

Yellow Sea

East China Sea

South China Sea

Java

Ocean

**Visit www.hoopoekids.com
for a complete list of Hoopoe titles, CDs, DVDs,
an introduction to the use of Teaching-Stories™
and parent/teacher guides.**

First Edition 2006

HOOPOE

Published by Hoopoe Books,
a division of The Institute for the Study of Human Knowledge

ISBN 1-883536-42-1

Library of Congress Cataloging-in-Publication Data

Shah, Idries, 1924-
    Fatima the spinner and the tent / written by Idries Shah ; [illustrated by Natasha Delmar].-- 1st ed.
        p. cm.
    Summary: When a series of misfortunes finally bring her to China where she is asked to make a tent for the
Emperor, Fatima comes to realize the value of all her past experiences in helping her forge a new and happier
life.
    ISBN 1-883536-42-1 (hdbk)
    [1. Folklore.] 1. Delmar, Natasha, ill. II. Title.

PZ8.1 .S47 Fat 2006
398.22--dc22

                                                                                                          2005031631

# FATIMA THE SPINNER AND THE TENT

written by
Idries Shah

HOOPOE BOOKS
BOSTON

Once, in a city in the Farthest West, there lived a girl called Fatima. She was the daughter of a prosperous spinner, who taught her to spin.

One day her father said to her, "Come, daughter, we are going on a journey, for I have business in the islands of the Middle Sea. Perhaps you may find some handsome youth in a good situation whom you could take as husband."

They set off and traveled from island to island, the father doing his trading while Fatima dreamt of the husband who might soon be hers.

One day, however, they were on the way to Crete when a storm blew up, and the ship was wrecked.

Fatima, only half conscious, was cast up on the seashore near Alexandria. Her father was drowned, and she was utterly destitute.

She could only remember dimly her life until then, for her experience of the shipwreck and her exposure in the sea had exhausted her.

While she was wandering on the sands, a family of weavers found her. Although they were poor, they took her into their humble home and taught her their craft.

Thus it was that she made a second life for herself, and within a year or two she was happy and reconciled to her lot.

But one day, when she was on the seashore for some reason, a band of slave-traders landed and carried her, along with other captives, away with them.

Although she bitterly lamented her new situation, Fatima found no sympathy from her captors, who took her to Istanbul to sell her as a slave.

Her world had collapsed for a second time.

Now it chanced that there were few buyers at the market. One of them was a man who was looking for slaves to work in his woodyard, where he made masts for ships.

When he saw the dejection of the unfortunate Fatima, he decided to buy her. He thought that in this way, at least, he might be able to give her a slightly better life than if she were bought by someone else.

He took Fatima to his home, intending to make her a serving-maid for his wife.

When he arrived at the house, however, he found that he had lost all his money in a ship's cargo which had been captured by pirates. He could not afford workers, so he, Fatima and his wife were left alone to work at the heavy labor of making masts.

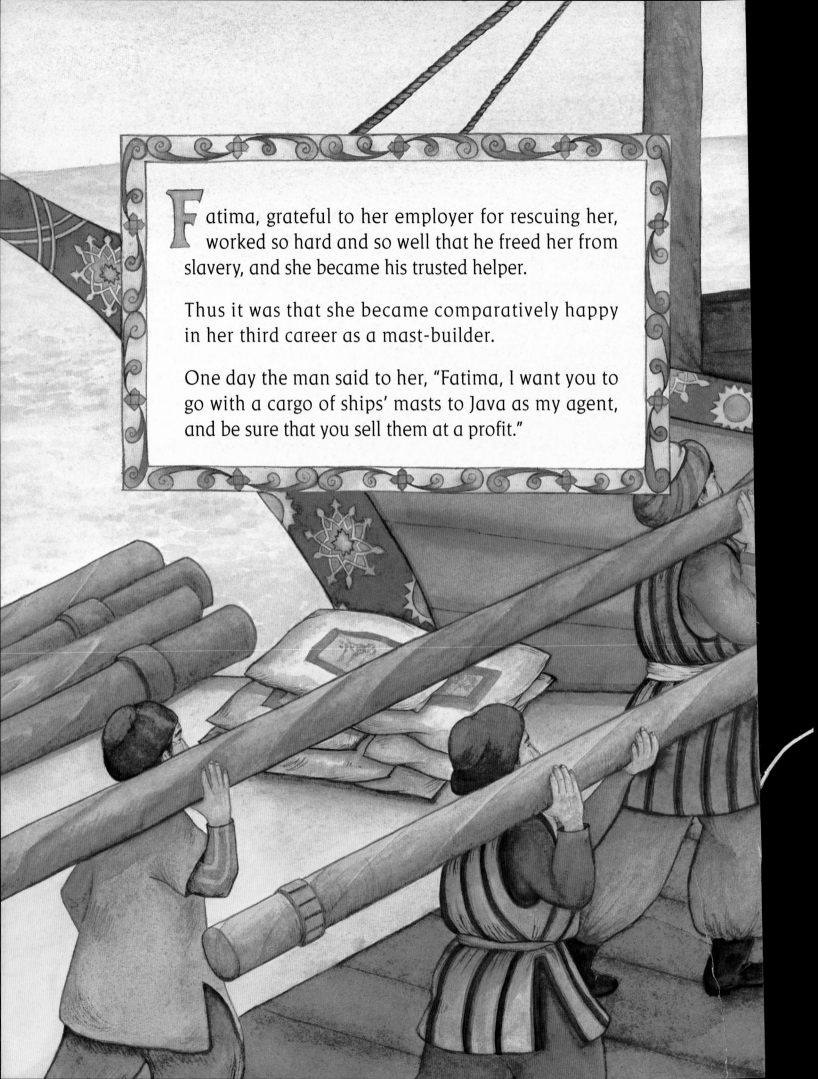

Fatima, grateful to her employer for rescuing her, worked so hard and so well that he freed her from slavery, and she became his trusted helper.

Thus it was that she became comparatively happy in her third career as a mast-builder.

One day the man said to her, "Fatima, I want you to go with a cargo of ships' masts to Java as my agent, and be sure that you sell them at a profit."

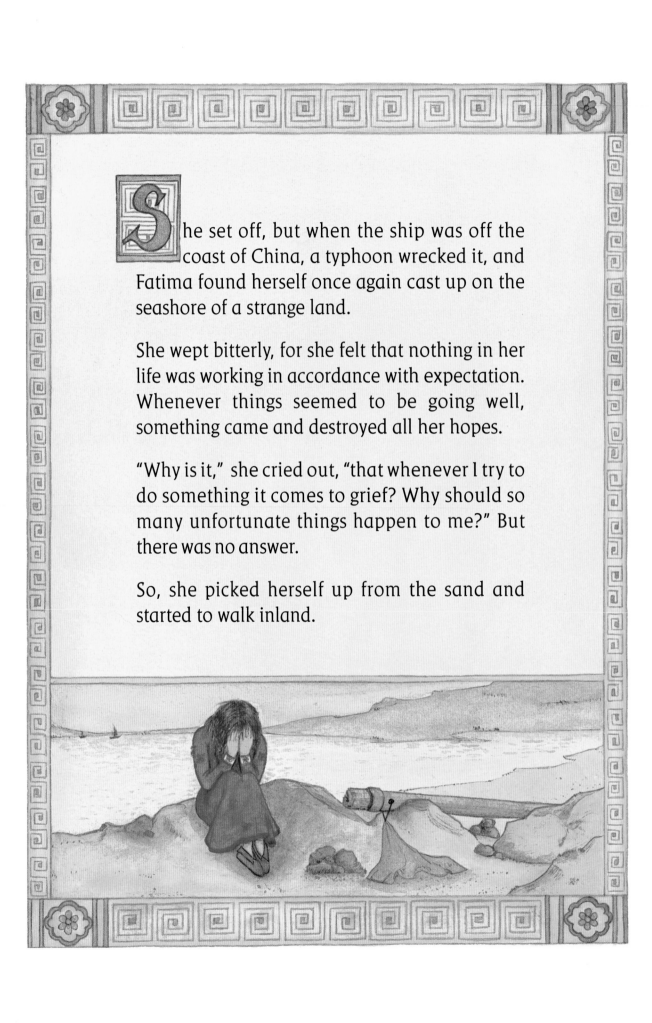

She set off, but when the ship was off the coast of China, a typhoon wrecked it, and Fatima found herself once again cast up on the seashore of a strange land.

She wept bitterly, for she felt that nothing in her life was working in accordance with expectation. Whenever things seemed to be going well, something came and destroyed all her hopes.

"Why is it," she cried out, "that whenever I try to do something it comes to grief? Why should so many unfortunate things happen to me?" But there was no answer.

So, she picked herself up from the sand and started to walk inland.

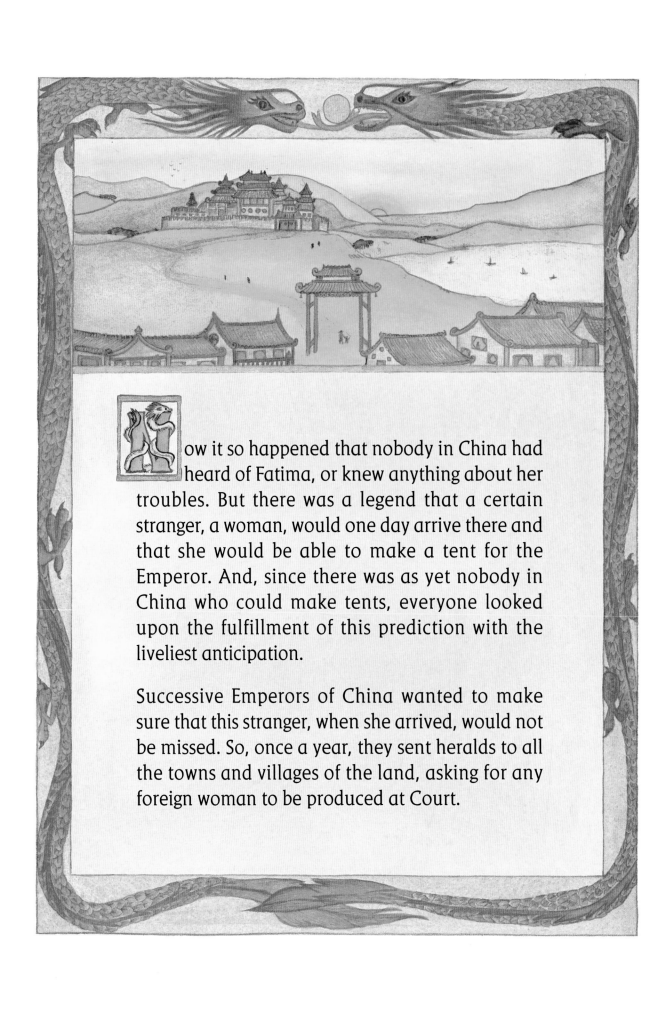

ow it so happened that nobody in China had heard of Fatima, or knew anything about her troubles. But there was a legend that a certain stranger, a woman, would one day arrive there and that she would be able to make a tent for the Emperor. And, since there was as yet nobody in China who could make tents, everyone looked upon the fulfillment of this prediction with the liveliest anticipation.

Successive Emperors of China wanted to make sure that this stranger, when she arrived, would not be missed. So, once a year, they sent heralds to all the towns and villages of the land, asking for any foreign woman to be produced at Court.

hen Fatima stumbled into a town by the seashore, it was one such occasion.

The people spoke to her through an interpreter and explained that she would have to go to see the Emperor.

ady," said the Emperor, when Fatima was brought before him, "can you make a tent?"

"I think so," said Fatima.

She asked for rope, but there was none to be had.

So, remembering her time as a spinner, she collected flax and made ropes.

Then she asked for strong cloth, but the Chinese had none of the kind that she needed. So, drawing on her experience with the weavers of Alexandria, she made some sturdy tent-cloth.

Then she found that she needed tent-poles, but there were none in China. So, Fatima, remembering how she had been trained by the mast-builder of Istanbul, cunningly made strong tent-poles.

When these were ready, she racked her brains for the memory of all the tents she had seen in her travels...

And Lo... a tent was made!

When this wonder was revealed to the Emperor of China, he offered Fatima the fulfillment of any wish she cared to name. She chose to settle in China, where she married a handsome prince, and where she remained in happiness, surrounded by her children, until the end of her days.